Why does fire come from a volcano?

Written by Sally Morgan

Illustrated by Victor Tavares

Collins

What's in this book?

Listen and say

Download the audio at www.collins.co.uk/839719

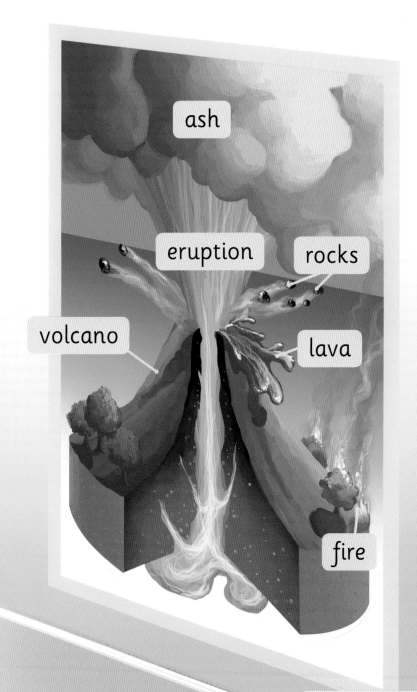

ash

eruption

rocks

volcano

lava

fire

Paul and his mother are shopping. They see a picture in a shop window.

"Look at the fire!" says Paul. "Is it from a dragon, Mum?"

"It's not from a dragon," says Mum. "That's a volcano."

"Why does fire come from a volcano?" asks Paul.

There are volcanoes in many different countries. A volcano is a big mountain. We cannot see all of the volcano because parts of it are under the sea.

In an old story from Italy, a man called Vulcan made the volcanoes. The word *volcano* comes from his name.

Sometimes, very hot rocks fly from the volcano. This is an *eruption*. Why is this?

eruption

Take a bottle of fizzy water.
Shake the bottle. Open it and lots of water
comes out.

fizzy water

There are many rocks under a volcano and they are very, very hot. They fly from the volcano, like the water from the bottle.

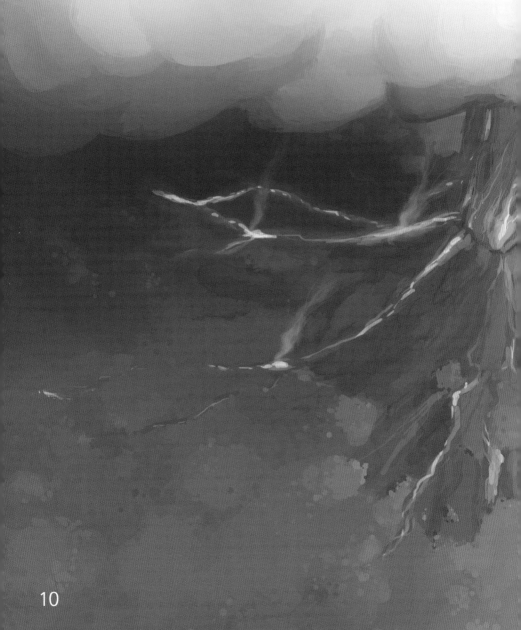

Rivers of red rock cross the ground.
This rock is called lava. You cannot go
near lava because it's very, very hot.

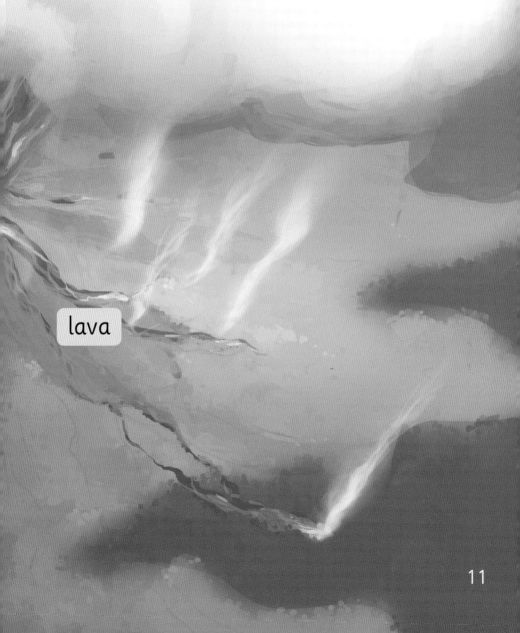

lava

This lava is crossing a road.
Sometimes the lava is slow and sometimes it's fast. Be very careful, it's not safe!

There's lots of noise in an eruption.
The eruption throws rocks into the air.
There's a lot of ash, too.

ash

Some eruptions are very big. The ground moves. Grey ash falls on many things. Can you see the ash on the car?

These trees are on the ground. There are no people here. The people moved to safe places.

After an eruption, the lava can get cold. It changes from red to black. You can walk on the black rock. It's safe.

Nothing grows on lava for many years. Then small plants start to grow. Can you see the orange plants? These plants like the lava.

Krakatoa is a famous volcano in the country Indonesia. In 1883, the eruption of Krakatoa was very loud. People in different countries talked about the noise it made!

Big waves from the sea near Krakatoa
went to a lot of different countries.
The sky was black for many weeks, too.
There was a lot of ash from the volcano.

Let's make a small volcano! Do this in the garden with a parent.

Make sand into the shape of a volcano.

Put a cup in the top of your volcano.

Add water, baking soda, soap and paint.
Then add the vinegar and watch.
Was there an eruption?

Picture dictionary

Listen and repeat

ash

eruption

fire

fizzy water

lava

shake

volcano

wave

1 Look and say "*Yes*" or "*No*"

Lava comes from a volcano.

Red lava is very hot.

You can walk on red lava.

Black lava is not very hot.

Plants cannot grow on lava.

2 Listen and say

Collins

Published by Collins
An imprint of HarperCollins*Publishers*
Westerhill Road
Bishopbriggs
Glasgow
G64 2QT

HarperCollins*Publishers*
1st Floor, Watermarque Building
Ringsend Road
Dublin 4
Ireland

William Collins' dream of knowledge for all began with the publication of his first book in 1819.

A self-educated mill worker, he not only enriched millions of lives, but also founded a flourishing publishing house. Today, staying true to this spirit, Collins books are packed with inspiration, innovation and practical expertise. They place you at the centre of a world of possibility and give you exactly what you need to explore it.

© HarperCollins*Publishers* Limited 2020

10 9 8 7 6 5 4 3 2

ISBN 978-0-00-839719-7

Collins® and COBUILD® are registered trademarks of HarperCollins*Publishers* Limited

www.collins.co.uk/elt

British Library Cataloguing in Publication Data

A catalogue record for this publication is available from the British Library.

Author: Sally Morgan
Illustrator: Victor Tavares (Beehive)
Series editor: Rebecca Adlard
Commissioning editor: Zoë Clarke
Publishing manager: Lisa Todd
Product managers: Jennifer Hall and Caroline Green
In-house editor: Alma Puts Keren
Project manager: Emily Hooton
Editor: Matthew Hancock
Proofreaders: Natalie Murray and Michael Lamb
Cover designer: Kevin Robbins
Typesetter: 2Hoots Publishing Services Ltd
Audio produced by id audio, London
Reading guide author: Emma Wilkinson
Production controller: Rachel Weaver
Printed and bound by: GPS Group, Slovenia

Download the audio for this book and a reading guide for parents and teachers at www.collins.co.uk/839719